Fairy

Level 2

Contents

Published by
Kuldeep Jain
for
Pegasus
An imprint of
B. Jain Publishers (P) Ltd.
1921, Street No. 10, Chuna Mandi, Paharganj, New Delhi-110055 (INDIA)
Phones: 91-11-4567 1000 | Fax: 91-11-4567 1010
Website: **www.bjain.com** | E-mail: **info@bjain.com**

Snow White and The Seven dwarfs

Let's know about Grimms Brothers

Snow White and The Seven Dwarfs was written by Jacob and Wilhelm Grimm known as the **Grimms Brothers**. They were writers from Germany who are remembered for their memorable contribution in fairy tales. The Grimms brothers had been collecting fairy tales from the people of Hesse since the early 1800s. In 1812, they got their first volume of eighty-six stories published. In 1814 the second volume containing seventy stories came.

Once upon a time, there lived a king and queen who longed for a child. One snowy morning, the queen sat stitching by her window. As she was stitching, she pricked her finger.

Just then, a thought came to her mind. 'I wish I had a daughter whose complexion would be as white as the snow outside with cheeks as red as this blood.

New Words | stitching
complexion

Her hair would be black like this ebony windowpane!'

After a few months the king and queen were blessed with a beautiful daughter who looked exactly as the queen had thought. She was white as snow, had red cheeks and black hair like the ebony wood! 'I will call her Snow White,' said the king, joyously.

However, the king's happiness was short lived, for the queen passed away soon after the princess was born. After some time, the king remarried. The new queen was extremely proud of her beauty. She even owned a magic mirror. Often she asked it,

New Words | ebony
windowpane
proud

'Mirror, Mirror, on the wall Who's the fairest of them all?'

When the mirror said, *'It's you, my queen.'* She was content.

Years passed by and Snow White grew up to be far more beautiful and fairer than the queen. One day, the queen asked the mirror the same question but the mirror replied,

'You, my Queen, are fair, But Snow White is fairer still.'

The queen was shocked and angry to hear this reply. She became jealous of Snow White's beauty.

The new queen began thinking of ways of how to get rid of Snow White. One day, the queen called a hunter and ordered him, 'Take Snow White to the forest and kill her. Remember to bring back her heart as a token of her death.'

New Words | jealous
shocked

The hunter was shocked when he heard the queen's command. As it was the queen's order, he had to take Snow White to the forest, though unwillingly.

New Words | unwillingly

Once inside the forest, the hunter who was kind and pitiful said to Snow White, 'Princess, the queen has ordered me to kill you but I can't do such a thing.'

Snow White was very frightened and asked, 'What do I do now?' 'Run deep into the forest and never show your face to the queen again,' replied the hunter.

So, Snow White ran deep into the forest never to return. Meanwhile, the hunter killed a rabbit, and took its heart to show the queen. 'I hope the queen believes me that it is the heart of Snow White.'

The queen was very pleased to see the rabbit's heart. 'Good work hunter!

New Words | pitiful
frightened

I'm pleased that you have done your work so particularly,' said the wicked queen, happily.

Meanwhile, Snow White walked on and on deep into the forest. She was very tired. 'O God! This forest is getting deeper and deeper and I think I am lost! My legs are aching too,' thought the poor girl.

But she walked on, in fear that evening would fall. After walking for a long time, she saw a pretty little cottage and began walking towards it. She knocked at the door.

'Is anybody there?' But no one answered. After a little thought, she went inside.

New Words | wicked
aching
knocked

Snow White was surprised to see that most of the furniture in the cottage was seven in number. There were seven tiny chairs at the dining table, seven arm chairs

New Words | furniture

in the drawing room and seven little beds in the bedroom! But the cottage was in a terrible mess. She decided to put everything back in order and tidy up the cottage. She cleaned up the whole place and by evening she was exhausted. Snow White lay down on a bed and soon felt asleep.

Now, this little cottage belonged to seven dwarfs, who had gone to work in the mines. When they returned to their cottage they were surprised to find their cottage spick and span and wondered who had done it.

'I wonder who has cleaned up our cottage within a day!' said one. 'You are so right. We should find out,' said

New Words	exhausted	spick and span
	terrible	mess

another. They searched for a while and were surprised to find a beautiful, young girl fast asleep on one of the beds.

New Words | searched
surprised

Next morning, when Snow White woke up, she was frightened to see the seven dwarfs. But when she saw their smiling faces, her fear disappeared. She told them how she had reached their cottage.

New Words | disappeared

Then, the eldest dwarf said, 'Princess, you can stay here as long as you wish to. But on one condition—you will keep our cottage clean and tidy.'

Snow white readily agreed to this. However, the dwarfs warned Snow White saying, 'The queen will soon realise that you are alive. Do not open the door for anyone.' Snow White decided that it was safer that way and started living with them.

Meanwhile, the wicked queen lived happily in her palace. One day, she asked her magical mirror again her favourite question. But to her shock, the mirror told her that Snow White, who lived with the dwarfs, was the fairest of all!

New Words | condition
favourite

The queen was very angry when she heard this. 'How can this be? Didn't the hunter kill her? I will severely punish him,' she said to herself.

Quickly, she dressed as a countrywoman and went towards the dwarfs' cottage in the forest with a basket full of apples. She had cleverly poisoned one apple in the basket.

In no time, the queen found out the dwarfs' cottage. Hurriedly, she knocked on the door and asked, 'Dear, would you like to buy some apples?' Snow White looked out of the window and said, 'No, thank you. I don't need apples.' 'My dear girl, look how delicious these apples look! To assure you that these apples are fine, I will take a bite from one,' said the queen.

New Words | severely

Saying this, she herself took a bite from an apple. Snow White could no longer resist the delicious looking apples. She asked for one. The queen, cleverly gave the poisoned apple to Snow White.

No sooner had Snow White taken a bite of the apple, she fell down. The queen was thrilled by her success and said happily, 'Now, I am the fairest of them all.'

Quickly, she returned to the castle, happy. Later that day, when the dwarfs returned, they found Snow White lying dead. 'Snow White, our dear friend, please do not leave us and go!' cried one. 'We will surely find out who killed our Snow White!' said another.

New Words	poisoned	delicious	resist
	thrilled	success	castle

The dwarfs loved Snow White so much that instead of burying her, they kept her inside a glass coffin. 'It seems

New Words | dwarfs

our dear Snow White is in a deep sleep and will wake up any moment,' they said to each other. They decorated the glass coffin with beautiful flowers. The dwarfs cried uncontrollably and didn't leave the glass coffin alone. There were always some of the dwarfs guarding the glass coffin in turns. They prayed and hoped for a miracle that would bring their dear Snow White back to life.

Days passed by but nothing much happened. One day, a prince had lost his way in the forest while hunting. He passed by the dwarfs' cottage and saw Snow White in her glass coffin. The prince got down from his horse and gazed at Snow White. He could not believe that anybody could

New Words | coffin uncontrollably gazed miracle

be so very beautiful. Instantly, he fell in love with her. He bent down and kissed the pretty girl's frozen brow. As it was a kiss of true love, Snow White stirred as if from a dream. She slowly got up.

New Words | frozen
stirred

Seeing this, the dwarfs came running. They thanked the prince. The prince married Snow White and he took her off to his palace of course with the dwarfs' permission. There in the palace, they lived happily for many years.

New Words | permission

Let's Recall

1. What did the Queen wish for one snowy morning?
2. Did her wish come true? What name did the king and the queen think for their daughter? Why?
3. What did the king do after the queen died suddenly?
4. How was the new queen? What magical object did she have? What did she use it for?
5. Whom did the new Queen call one day and what task did she give him?
6. After leaving the palace, whom did Snow White live with?
7. How did she die?
8. Who saved her life in the end?

Little Red Riding Hood

Let's know about Grimms Brothers

Little Red Riding Hood was written by Jacob and Wilhelm Grimm known as the **Grimms Brothers**. They were writers from Germany who are remembered for their memorable contribution in fairy tales. The Grimms brothers had been collecting fairy tales from the people of Hesse since the early 1800s. In 1812, they got their first volume of eighty-six stories published. In 1814 the second volume containing seventy stories came.

Long ago, there lived a little girl with her mother near the edge of a forest. On her birthday, the little girl's grandmother had gifted her a beautiful red cape with a hood. 'My dear, I have made this red cape for you. You will look very pretty when you wear this,' said the old lady. 'O thank you grandmother! It is indeed very nice of you to bring this for me,' said the little girl, happily.

New Words | edge
cape

The little girl liked the red cape so very much that she wore it very often. And due to this, in her neighbourhood she came to be known as 'Little Red Riding Hood'.

One day, Red Riding Hood's mother said, 'Dear, your grandmother is ill. Please take this basket of cookies to her.' 'Very well, mother,' replied Little Red Riding Hood.

'But remember, don't stray from your path and don't talk to strangers,' warned her mother. 'I will remember all this mother. Do not worry for me,' said Little Red Riding Hood.

Now, Little Riding Hood's grandmother lived in a small cottage on the other side of

New Words | neighbourhood
strangers

the forest. So, Little Red Riding Hood had to cross the forest.

As she was completely unaware of the dangers of a forest, she skipped merrily along the forest path. Many beautiful butterflies flitted by her and the little girl, charmed by their beauty, followed them. 'What amazingly colourful butterflies! I have never seen such lovely creatures before,' said Little Red Riding Hood to herself, as she followed them.

After a long walk, Little Red Riding Hood reached a valley of colourful flowers. 'Oh! What pretty flowers! Let me collect some for my grandmother,' said Red Riding Hood to herself.

Just then, she saw a wolf standing beside her. 'Little girl, what are you doing

New Words | skipped unaware charmed creatures valley

in the forest?' he asked. 'My grandmother is ill. I am going to visit her with a basket of cookies and some flowers,' replied Red Riding Hood, confidently.

When the wolf heard this, a wicked thought struck his mind. Now, this wolf who stayed in this forest and ate smaller animals, was known for his cunningness.

Since many days, the cunning wolf did not have any proper meal. So he happily thought, 'Here is a good catch!'

He made an innocent face and asked the little girl, 'Where does your grandmother live, child?' 'The little cottage near the brook belongs to my grandmother,' replied the girl.

New Words | confidently
cunningness

Then, the crafty wolf said, 'Little girl, I think your grandmother will love the sweet strawberries growing deep in the woods. Will you pick some for her?'

New Words | crafty

'What a wonderful idea! Of course I would love pick up some for her. But dear wolf, which way shall I go?' asked the poor girl. 'O don't worry dear. Go straight and then turn right and then left and just at the corner, you will find the strawberries growing!' said the wolf, happily.

In this way, the cunning wolf made little Red Riding Hood stray further from the path.

'Now, I should rush to the cottage. A delicious meal awaits me,' cried out the wolf with joy.

Now the wicked wolf knew a shorter path through the forest to reach the brook. Soon the wolf was running at a high speed

New Words | brook

through the forest path. And within minutes, he reached the little cottage which belonged to Red Riding Hood's grandmother. The wolf knocked at the door of the cottage.

New Words | knocked

‘Who is it?’ asked Red riding Hood’s grandmother.

‘It’s, Little Red Riding Hood, grandmother,’ said the wolf, trying to sound like the little girl. ‘Child, I’m too weak to open the door. Lift the latch and come in,’ said grandmother.

Without wasting a moment, the wolf stepped inside the cottage. He saw grandma lying in bed. ‘O where are you my dear girl Come closer to me. Let me see you my dear,’ said the old lady. ‘Coming grandmother, coming,’ said the cunning wolf.

Quickly, the wolf jumped on to the bed, and gobbled up grandmother greedily!

New Words | latch
gobbled

Then, he dressed himself in her clothes and lay down in her bed waiting for Little Red Riding Hood.

Meanwhile, Little Red Riding Hood gathered plenty of strawberries. After Little Red Riding Hood had filled her basket with juicy strawberries, she met some woodcutters. She told them about the wolf. The woodcutters were surprised that the wolf hadn't attacked her.

Soon, she reached her granny's cottage and knocked at the door. The wolf feigned the voice of her grandmother and said, 'Child, lift the latch and come in.'

Snow White did as she was told. She was a bit surprised by her grandmother's voice as she welcomed her quite formally.

However, Little Red Riding Hood went near her bed to talk to her

New Words | attacked
feigned

grandmother. When, the little girl looked at her grandmother, she cried, 'Grandma, what happened to your hands? They are covered with hair!'

'Child, I had been gathering chestnuts for you, and the burrs stuck to my fingers,' replied the wolf. 'What big eyes you have!' she said. 'All the better to see you with,' replied the wolf.

Now, Little Red Riding Hood came a step nearer to the wolf and asked, 'Grandma, what a black nose you have!' 'All the better to smell the cookies in your basket,' replied the disguised wolf.

The more Red Riding Hood gazed at her grandmother, the more she was

New Words | burrs
disguised
gazed

surprised. 'Grandma, what large teeth you have!' 'All the better to eat you with!' cried the wolf.

With these words, the wolf jumped off the bed and gobbled up Little Red Riding Hood.

After eating his fill, the wolf fell asleep. Meanwhile, one of the woodcutters whom Little Red Riding Hood had met, was passing by the cottage. He thought, 'Why

is the place so quiet? With a little girl in the house, there should be some noises. Let me take a look.'

With this thought, the woodcutter went inside the cottage. What the woodcutter saw on entering the cottage was something which he had never thought of!

He saw the wolf sleeping merrily on the bed dressed in grandmother's clothes. At once, he understood everything.

Without wasting a moment, he took a pair of scissors and began to cut open the stomach of the wolf. After two snips, there was a big hole in the wolf's stomach and Little Red Riding Hood jumped out! 'How dark it was inside! Thank you very much Sir for saving me.'

New Words | scissors

'My dear girl, the wolf had eaten YOU? How awful it must have been being inside the wolf's belly!' said the woodcutter.

'Where is your grandmother whom you were coming to meet?' asked the woodcutter, puzzled. Two more snips in the wolf's tummy brought out grandmother too. 'O grandmother, are you all right?' cried Red riding Hood happily. 'Yes my child! I cannot believe that we are safe!' said grandmother, surprised.

After this, the woodcutter filled the wolf's stomach with large stones and stitched it properly. And then, they hid near the cottage waiting for the wolf to wake up.

New Words | awful, stitched, stomach, puzzled

When the wolf woke up, he walked unsteadily towards the brook to drink water. As he bent down to drink water, he lost his balance, tumbled and was drowned.

At once, the woodcutter, Red Riding Hood and her grandmother came out of their hiding place. They sat down and enjoyed the cookies that Little Red Riding Hood's mother had packed. 'Thanks to you for saving our lives sir,' said Red Riding Hood's grandmother to the woodcutter. The little girl promised her grandmother, 'From now on, I will always obey my elders. I will never talk to strangers.'

New Words

tumbled
unsteadily
drowned
obey
promised

Since that day, Little Red Riding Hood didn't wander away from the path in the forest, neither for flowers nor for strawberries.

Let's Recall

1. What did the little Red Riding Hood's grandma gift her?
2. Where did Red Riding Hood's mother send her one day? Why?
3. Whom did she meet on the way?
4. What suggestion did the wolf give her?
5. When Red Riding Hood reached her grandma's house what happened?
6. Who saved Red Riding Hood and her grandma from the wolf?
7. Describe briefly how he saved them.

Goldilocks and The Three Bears

Let's know about Robert Southey

The Story of the Three Bears or Goldilocks and the Three Bears is an **English fairy tale** first written in a narrative form by a British author and poet, **Robert Southey**.

Robert Southey was an English poet of the Romantic school. Southey's fame has been long hidden by his powerful and well-known contemporaries and friends like William Wordsworth and Samuel Taylor Coleridge.

As a literary person, Southey was a productive letter writer, literary scholar, essay writer, historian and biographer. He was also a renowned Portuguese and Spanish scholar, translating a number of works of those two countries into English. He also wrote the *History of Brazil* and a *History of the Peninsular War.* Perhaps Southey's most powerful contribution to literature is the children's classic, *The Story of the Three Bears.*

Long ago, there lived a pretty little girl named Goldilocks. Goldilocks had beautiful golden locks of hair. That is why she was called 'Goldilocks'. She lived in a lovely cottage with her parents. Their cottage was located near the woods and Goldilocks loved to explore it.

One day, Goldilocks wanted to go to the woods alone to gather wild flowers.

New Words | explore

'Be home by dinner time,' said her mother, when she was going out. 'Yes mother,' replied Goldilocks, planning in her mind to go further into the woods than she had been before.

Goldilocks wandered deep into the woods. She skipped all her way looking at the tall trees, colourful flowers and listening to the twittering of the birds. After quite sometime the little girl realized that she had gone deep into the forest and had lost her way.

Goldilocks was worried and she thought, 'How will I return home? Mother will be waiting for me!' Little did she realise that she had almost reached the other side of the forest.

New Words | skipped
twittering

Now, in that same forest lived a family of three bears in a pretty little cottage. At the time when Goldilocks was lost and was trying to find her way out in the forest, this bear family was sitting for their dinner.

'Mom, the porridge is too hot!' said Baby Bear, when he tried to eat a spoonful. 'Is that so or are you making an excuse! Let me see for myself,' said Father Bear. 'Yes, it's really hot!' he cried, when he tried eating it.

'What shall we do now?' cried Baby Bear. 'Let's go out for a walk. The porridge will cool down by the time we return,' suggested Father Bear. 'I think that's a very good idea,' said Mother Bear.

New Words | porridge
excuse
suggested

So, the three bears set out for a walk. Thinking that they'd walk near their house and would return in a few moments, Mother Bear did not lock the door behind her.

A few minutes later when the three Bears were out for a walk, Goldilocks reached the charming little cottage which belonged to the Bear family. She peeped

New Words | charming
peeped

in through the window but couldn't see anybody.

'Let me find out who stays here,' she thought and went to the other side of the cottage, looking for the door. Goldilocks knocked gently at the open door and asked, 'Hello! Is anyone home?' When she got no reply she pushed the door and it opened. 'O my, my! Was the door open?'

Saying this, she stepped into the cottage. The cottage was beautifully decorated. It was very neat too.

Goldilocks moved from one room to another. She had seen the bedroom and immediately after that she reached the dinning room. She noticed three bowls

New Words | knocked
decorated

filled with porridge on the table. At once, Goldilocks realised that she was very hungry. 'The porridge looks delicious,' she said to herself. 'Let me eat some!'

She took a spoonful from the big bowl and screamed, for the porridge was too hot. She tried some from the middle-sized bowl which belonged to the Mother Bear. 'Oh! This is too cold,' she cried out. Then she picked up the small bowl and tasted the porridge from it. 'Mmm, this is just right,' she said and finished the porridge.

After finishing off the porridge Goldilocks wished to see the rest of the cottage. So, she began moving around

New Words | delicious
porridge
screamed

the house again and finally reached the living room.

She was delighted to see the living room. There were three chairs—a large one, a medium one and a small one. Long hours of walking had made the little girl tired. She was tempted to rest for some time. 'I am too tired to do anything right now. I think I should rest a while,' thought Goldilocks. At first, she tried to sit on Father Bear's chair.

'This chair is too high,' she cried.

Next, she sat on Mother Bear's chair. 'Oh! This one is too wide,' she said. Lastly, she tried sitting on Baby Bear's chair. 'This one is just perfect. Let me sit on it and rest for a while,' she said and sat on it. But sadly, the chair broke and Goldilocks fell down.

New Words

delighted
medium
tempted

'O dear! I broke the chair and I hurt myself too. Never mind, there must be some other place where I can rest.'

Saying this, she got up, dusted her clothes and went ahead to explore the rest of the cottage.

By that time, Goldilocks was very tired. 'I need to sleep for a while,' she

New Words | explore

thought and started searching for the bedroom. In the bedroom, she saw three beds. She climbed onto the biggest bed as it was large and looked comfortable. But how wrong she was in her thinking!

'This bed is so hard,' said Goldilocks and got down. Then she tried getting into Mother Bear's bed. 'Let me try this medium bed,' she said to herself. But to her dismay, this bed was too soft for her. 'I think I should try that tiny bed,' she thought, when she saw the Baby Bear's bed.

So, she climbed onto this bed and lay down happily. 'Perfect! This bed is just right,' Goldilocks cried and in no time, she was fast asleep.

New Words | perfect
medium
dismay

A little later, the three bears returned. They were really hungry after their walk. 'I am really hungry now due to our long walk,' said Father Bear. They rushed to the dining room to have their meal of porridge. When Father Bear looked into his large bowl, he growled, 'Who has eaten my porridge?' Then Mother Bear cried, 'Someone has eaten my porridge too.'

Baby Bear wailed, 'SOMEBODY HAS FINISHED MY PORRIDGE! Now what will I eat? BOO! BOO!'

As the Baby Bear had begun crying violently, Mother Bear was busy making him quiet. 'It is all right my baby! You can share our porridge,' she said fondly.

New Words | growled
violently

Tired and hungry, they sat down at the dining table and the three shared the remaining porridge. After they had had their dinner, the family went into towards the living room. 'Let's sit for a while and talk to our little son,' said Father Bear and they walked to their living room. They were surprised again. 'Somebody has been sitting on my chair!' growled Father Bear. 'Somebody has been sitting on my chair too!' cried Mother Bear. 'Somebody sat on my chair and has BROKEN it too!' cried out Baby Bear, with tears in his eyes.

Again, Mother Bear had a difficult time making her baby quiet. As they were already tired, the Bear family decided to go to their bedroom upstairs, to sleep.

New Words | growled

When Father Bear looked at his bed, he saw that the bed spread had been badly crumpled. He at once shouted, 'Who has been sleeping on my bed?' When Mother Bear noticed the wrinkled sheets on her bed, she screamed also.

'Who has been sleeping on my bed? Look at the state of my bed!'

New Words | crumpled
wrinkled

All that time, Goldilocks was lost in a world of dreams. She dreamt of honey bees buzzing around her. She saw that she had become friendly with a bunny rabbit. 'Can you show me the way to my home bunny? I think I am lost!' she said in her dream.

Suddenly her dream was broken when Baby Bear cried, 'LOOK! Somebody is sleeping in my bed and she is still there!'

The Baby Bear's voice woke up Goldilocks. She was startled to see the three angry bears standing near her beside the bed looking down at her.

The bears were also very surprised to see Goldilocks. Father Bear cried, 'How could she come into our cottage. Did

New Words | startled
buzzing

you not lock the door?' Baby Bear said longingly, 'She is so cute! Can't she be my friend?' And Mother Bear was too surprised to say anything. She kept on gazing at Goldilocks as she had never seen such a pretty girl before!

New Words | longingly

Goldilocks got down from the bed. Though she was tired and sleepy, she did not waste a minute. She put on her shoes and cap, climbed downstairs and fled from the cottage. The Baby Bear, who always wanted to have a friend, ran after her. He kept asking her if she would be his friend but, Goldilocks being too frightened continued to run and soon disappeared in the woods.

'Pretty girl, please do not run away! Please be my friend and play with me,' he pleaded.

But Goldilocks ran and ran. She did not stop even for a minute and finally reached home, breathless but safe. Her mother, who was beginning to get worried

New Words | breathless

asked, 'Where were you, Goldilocks? Next time, you will not go to the forest alone.' Goldilocks did not argue and very gently said, 'Yes, Mother, as you say.' Goldilocks of course did not tell her mother why she agreed with her.

New Words | argue
agreed

Let's Recall

1. Why was the little girl in the story called Goldilocks?
2. Where did she go alone one day and why?
3. What happened there?
4. What did Goldilocks see inside the cottage in the forest?
5. Whom did the cottage belong to?
6. What did Goldilocks do in the cottage?
7. How did Goldilocks escape from the cottage?